Olde Tyme Mother Goose

Nursery Rhymes
and Folk Tales

Illustrated by
Frederick Richardson

★ A Tell-Me-A-Story Keepsake Treasury ★

Olde Tyme Mother Goose

Nursery Rhymes
and Folk Tales

Dalmatian Press

OLDE TYME MOTHER GOOSE NURSERY RHYMES *and* FOLK TALES
Copyright © 2004 Dalmatian Press, LLC

Editor: Louise Gikow
Cover Design: Emily Robertson
Text Design: Mark Weinberg

Published in 2004 by Dalmatian Press, LLC.
The DALMATIAN PRESS name and logo are trademarks
of Dalmatian Press, LLC, Franklin, Tennessee 37067.
No part of this book may be reproduced or copied in any form
without the written permission of Dalmatian Press.

ISBN: 1-40370-881-9
13404-0604

04 05 06 07 08 SFO 10 9 8 7 6 5 4 3 2 1

Tell Me A Story.

When you read a poem or story to your child, lots of good things happen. You show your child that reading is exciting and fun. You encourage the growth and development not just of your little one's imagination, but also his or her vocabulary, comprehension skills, and overall school readiness.

Research shows, time and time again, that children who are read to on a regular basis do significantly better in school than children who are not read to at home. We encourage you to spend ten to twenty minutes every day reading to your child. It's a small amount of quality time that reaps a big reward!

It's also important to keep reading books *to* your child and *with* your child even after he or she is reading independently. You can share books that are slightly more difficult than what your child is reading on his or her own because you are available to help with vocabulary words and any questions your child may have about the poem or story.

Read and Discuss.

No matter how old your child is, or how well she is reading independently, remember that story time is the perfect opportunity to talk about what you're reading and any other topics that might arise from it. This kind of dialog helps make stories come alive and adds depth to your child's reading experience.

What would you do if you were in the story? you might ask. *How might you fix this problem? Did the character do the right thing?* and so forth.

Your child's Keepsake Treasury includes dialogic questions throughout the stories to prompt meaningful and memorable conversations. Ask your own questions as well. You might be surprised at the imaginative discussions that follow. You can learn more about dialogic reading online at: *http://www.readingrockets.org.*

We hope that *Olde Tyme Mother Goose Nursery Rhymes and Folk Tales* will become a treasured part of your family's library.

Happy Reading!

CONTENTS

Hear What Ma'am Goose Says!

My dear little Blossoms, there are now in this world, and always will be, a great many grannies besides myself, both in petticoats and pantaloons, some a deal younger, to be sure, but all monstrous wise and of my own family name. These old women, who never had chick or child of their own, but who always know how to bring up other people's children, will tell you with long faces that my enchanting, quieting, soothing volume, my all-sufficient anodyne for cross, peevish, won't-be-comforted little children, ought be laid aside for more learned books, such as *they* could select and publish.

Nonsense! I tell you all their batterings can't deface my beauties nor their wiser pratings equal my wiser prattlings; and all imitators of my refreshing songs might as well write another Billy Shakespeare as another Mother Goose—we two great poets were born together, and shall go out of the world together.

No, no, my melodies will never die,
While nurses sing, or babies cry.

OLD MOTHER GOOSE

Old Mother Goose, when
    She wanted to wander,
Would ride through the air
    On a very fine gander.

Mother Goose had a house,
    'Twas built in a wood.
An owl at the door
    For a porter stood.

She had a son Jack,
    A plain-looking lad.
He was not very good,
    Nor yet very bad.

She sent him to market,
    A live goose he bought.
"Here! mother," says he,
    "It will not go for naught."

Jack's goose and her gander
    Grew very fond;
They'd both eat together,
    Or swim in one pond.

Jack found one morning,
    As I have been told,
His goose had laid him
    An egg of pure gold.

Jack rode to his mother,
    The news for to tell.
She called him a good boy
    And said it was well.

And Old Mother Goose
    The goose saddled soon,
And mounting its back,
    Flew up to the moon.

 After Mother Goose flies up to the moon, where do you think she will go next?

Old Mother Goose, when
She wanted to wander,
Would ride through the air
On a very fine gander.

Cock-a-doodle-doo,
My dame has lost her shoe.
My master's lost his fiddlestick,
And knows not what to do.

Peter, Peter, pumpkin eater,
Had a wife and couldn't keep her;
He put her in a pumpkin shell,
And then he kept her very well.

Peter, Peter, pumpkin eater,
Had another and didn't love her;
Peter learned to read and spell,
And then he loved her very well.

What a big pumpkin! How big is the biggest pumpkin you've ever seen?

One misty, moisty morning,
  When cloudy was the weather,
I chanced to meet an old man clothed all in leather.
He began to compliment, and I began to grin,
  How do you do, and how do you do?
  And how do you do again?

I had a little hobby-horse,
And it was dapple gray.
Its head was made of pea-straw,
Its tail was made of hay.
I sold it to an old woman
For a copper groat;
And I'll not sing my song again
Without another coat.

Monday's child is fair of face,
Tuesday's child is full of grace,
Wednesday's child is full of woe,
Thursday's child has far to go,
Friday's child is loving and giving,
Saturday's child works hard for a living;
But the child that is born on the Sabbath day
Is bonny and blithe and good and gay.

Mary had a little lamb
With fleece as white as snow.
And everywhere that Mary went
The lamb was sure to go.

It followed her to school one day—
That was against the rule.
It made the children laugh and play
To see a lamb at school.

And so the teacher turned it out,
But still it lingered near,
And waited patiently about
Till Mary did appear.

"Why does the lamb love Mary so?"
The eager children cry.
"Why, Mary loves the lamb, you know!"
The teacher did reply.

 What does a baby lamb say?
Have you ever seen a baby lamb?

Little Nanny Etticoat
In a white petticoat,
    And a red nose;
The longer she stands
    The shorter she grows.

This poem is a riddle. Do you know what little Nanny Etticoat is?*

* *She's a candle! Her flame is her "red nose"
and her wax is her "white petticoat."*

I like little kitty, her coat is so warm.
And if I don't hurt her she'll do me no harm.
So I'll not pull her tail, not drive her away,
But kitty and I very gently will play.

What do you like about kittens?

Little Bo-peep has lost her sheep,
And can't tell where to find them.
Leave them alone, and they'll come home,
And bring their tails behind them.

"Billy, Billy come and play,
While the sun shines bright as day."

"Yes, my Polly, so I will,
For I love to please you still."

"Billy, Billy, have you seen
Sam and Betsy on the green?"

"Yes, my Poll, I saw them pass,
Skipping o'er the new-mown grass."

Hie to the market, Jenny come trot,
Spilt all her buttermilk, every drop!
Every drop and every dram—
Jenny came home with an empty can.

Birds of a feather flock together,
And so will pigs and swine.
Rats and mice have their choice,
And so will I have mine.

My mother said that I never should
Play with the gypsies in the wood.
The wood was dark, the grass was green;
By came Sally with a tambourine.
I went to sea—no ship to get across;
I paid ten shillings for a blind white horse.
I upped on his back and was off in a crack,
Sally, tell my mother I shall never come back.

Pretty John Watts,
    We are troubled with rats.
Will you drive them out of the house?
    We have mice, too, in plenty,
    That feast in the pantry,
    But let them stay
    And nibble away.
What harm in a little brown mouse?

*How many gray mice
are in the picture?
Can you count them?*

I'll tell you a story
About Mary Morey,
And now my story's begun.
I'll tell you another
About her brother,
And now my story's done.

What is silly about this nursery rhyme?

Hush-a-bye, Baby, upon the tree top,
When the wind blows the cradle will rock;
When the bough breaks the cradle will fall,
Down tumbles cradle and Baby and all.

Ride away, ride away,
  Johnny shall ride,
And he shall have pussy-cat
  Tied to one side.
And he shall have little dog
  Tied to the other,
And Johnny shall ride
  To see his grandmother.

Go to bed first,
A golden purse;
Go to bed second,
A golden pheasant;
Go to bed third,
A golden bird.

There's a neat little clock,
In the schoolroom it stands,
And it points to the time
With its two little hands.

And may we, like the clock,
Keep a face clean and bright,
With hands ever ready
To do what is right.

A cat came fiddling out of a barn,
With a pair of bagpipes under her arm.
She could sing nothing but, "Fiddle-de-dee,
The mouse has married the bumble-bee."
Pipe, cat!
Dance, mouse!
We'll have a wedding at our good house.

Little Betty Blue
Lost her holiday shoe.
What will poor Betty do?
Why, give her another
To match the other,
And then she will walk in two.

Hickory, dickory, dock,
The mouse ran up the clock.
The clock struck one,
The mouse ran down,
Hickory, dickory, dock.

Can you tell what time it is on the big clock?

About the bush, Willie, about the bee-hive,
About the bush, Willie, I'll meet thee alive.

Little Tommy Tittlemouse
Lived in a little house.
He caught fishes
In other men's ditches.

A, B, C, D, E, F, G,
H, I, J, K, L, M, N,O, P,
Q, R, S and T, U, V,
W, X and Y and Z.
Now I've said my A B C,
Tell me what you think of me.

Three little kittens lost their
    mittens,
    And they began to cry,
    "Oh! mother dear, we very much
    fear
    That we have lost our mittens."
"Lost your mittens! You naughty
    kittens!
    Then you shall have have no pie."
      Mee-ow, mee-ow, mee-ow.
    "No, you shall have no pie."
      Mee-ow, mee-ow, mee-ow.

The three little kittens found their
    mittens
    And they began to cry,
    "Oh! mother dear, see here,
    see here,
    See, we have found our mittens."
"Put on your mittens, you silly
    kittens,
    And you may have some pie."
      Purr-r, purr-r, purr-r.
    "Oh! let us have the pie."
      Purr-r, purr-r, purr-r.

The three little kittens put on their
    mittens,
    And soon ate up the pie.
    "Oh! mother dear, we greatly
    fear
    That we have soiled our mittens."
"Soiled your mittens! You naughty
    kittens!"
    Then they began to sigh,
      Mee-ow, mee-ow, mee-ow.
    Then they began to sigh,
      Mee-ow, mee-ow, mee-ow.

The three little kittens washed their
    mittens
    And hung them out to dry.
    "Oh! mother dear, do you not hear,
    That we have washed our
    mittens?"
"Washed your mittens! Oh! you're
    good kittens,
    But I smell a rat close by."
      Hush! hush! Mee-ow, mee-ow.
    "We smell a rat close by."
      Mee-ow, mee-ow, mee-ow.

Blind man, blind man,
Sure you can't see?
Turn round three times,
And try to catch me.
Turn east, turn west,
Catch as you can,
Did you think you'd caught me?
Blind, blind man!

Shoe the colt,
Shoe the colt,
Shoe the wild mare.
Here a nail
There a nail,
Colt must go bare.

The little robin grieves
　　When the snow is on the ground,
For the trees have no leaves,
　　And no berries can be found.

The air is cold, the worms are hid;
　　For robin here what can be done?
Let's strow around some crumbs of bread,
　　And then he'll live till snow is gone.

Baa, baa, black sheep,
Have you any wool?
Yes, marry, have I,
Three bags full:
One for my master,
One for my dame,
But none for the little boy
Who cries in the lane.

*What would you make
if you had black wool?*

Hickety, pickety, my black hen,
She lays eggs for gentlemen.
Gentlemen come every day
To see what my black hen doth lay.

Wee Willie Winkie runs through the town,
Upstairs and downstairs, in his nightgown,
Tapping at the window, crying at the lock,
"Are the babes in their beds?— for now it's ten o'clock!"

What is your bedtime?

Three young rats with black felt hats,
Three young ducks with white straw flats,
Three young dogs with curling tails,
Three young cats with demi-veils,
Went out to walk with three young pigs
In satin vests and sorrel wigs.
But suddenly it chanced to rain
And so they all went home again.

See-saw, sacradown,
Which is the way to London town?
One foot up, the other foot down,
That is the way to London town.

Tweedle-dum and Tweedle-dee
Resolved to have a battle,
For Tweedle-dum said Tweedle-dee
Had spoiled his nice new rattle.
Just then flew by a monstrous crow,
As big as a tar barrel,
Which frightened both the heroes so,
They quite forgot their quarrel.

Bobby Shaftoe's gone to sea,
With silver buckles on his knee.
He'll come back to marry me,
    Pretty Bobby Shaftoe.

Bobby Shaftoe's fat and fair,
Combing down his yellow hair.
He's my love forevermore,
    Pretty Bobby Shaftoe.

There was a man and he had naught.
　　And robbers came to rob him.
He crept up to the chimney top,
　　And then they thought they had him.
But he got down on the other side,
　　And then they could not find him.
He ran fourteen miles in fifteen days,
　　And never looked back behind him.

Willie boy, Willie boy,
  Where are you going?
O, let us go with you
  This sunshiny day.

I'm going to the meadow
  To see them a-mowing,
I'm going to help the girls
  Turn the new hay.

Three children sliding on the ice
  Upon a summer's day,
As it fell out, they all fell in,
  The rest they ran away.

Oh, had these children been at school,
  Or sliding on dry ground,
Ten thousand pounds to one penny
  They had not then been drowned.

Ye parents who have children dear,
  And ye, too, who have none,
If you would keep them safe abroad,
  Pray keep them safe at home.

There was an old man,
And he had a calf,
And that's half.
He took him out of the stall,
And put him on the wall,
And that's all.

Can you say some words that rhyme with "all"?

There was a lady loved a swine.
"Honey," quoth she,
"Pig-hog wilt thou be mine?"
"Hoogh," quoth he.

"I'll build thee a silver sty,
Honey," quoth she,
"And in it though shalt lie."
"Hoogh," quoth he.

"Pinned with a silver pin,
Honey," quoth she,
"That thou may go out and in."
"Hoogh," quoth he.

"Wilt thou have me now,
Honey?" quoth she.
"Speak or my heart will break."
"Hoogh," quoth he.

If all the seas were one sea,
What a great sea that would be!
And if all the trees were one tree,
What a great tree that would be!
And if all the axes were one axe,
What a great axe that would be!
And if all the men were one man,
What a great man he would be!
And if the great man took the great axe,
And cut down the great tree,
And let it fall into the great sea,
What a splish splash that would be!

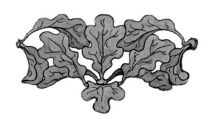

Thirty white horses upon a red hill,
Now they tramp, now they champ,
Now they stand still.

Here am I, little jumping Joan.
When nobody's with me
    I'm always alone.

*Who is with you
when you're alone?*

Bow, wow, wow!
Whose dog art thou?
Little Tom Tinker's dog,
Bow, wow, wow!

Simple Simon met a pieman
  Going to the fair.
Says Simple Simon to the pieman:
  "Pray let me taste your ware."

Says the pieman to Simple Simon:
  "Show me first your penny."
Says Simple Simon to the pieman:
  "Indeed I have not any."

There was an old woman lived under the hill,
And if she's not gone she lives there still.
Baked apples she sold and cranberry pies,
And she's the old woman that never told lies.

How many cranberry pies does old woman have to sell?

Robin Hood, Robin Hood,
Is in the mickle wood!
Little John, Little John,
He to the town is gone.

Robin Hood, Robin Hood,
Telling his beads,*
All in the greenwood
Among the green weeds.

Little John, Little John,
If he comes no more,
Robin Hood, Robin Hood,
We shall fret full sore!

Peter Piper picked a peck of pickled peppers;
A peck of pickled peppers Peter Piper picked.
If Peter Piper picked a peck of pickled peppers,
Where's the peck of pickled peppers Peter Piper picked?

* praying with his rosary beads

A wise old owl sat in an oak.
The more he heard the less he spoke;
The less he spoke the more he heard.
Why aren't we all like that wise old bird?

 *This is a poem about listening.*
Stop and listen for a moment.
What can you hear?

There was a little boy and a little girl
Lived in an alley.
Says the little boy to the little girl,
"Shall I, oh, shall I?"

Says the little girl to the little boy,
"What shall we do?"
Says the little boy to the little girl,
"I will kiss you."

To market, to market, to buy a fat pig,
Home again, home again, jiggety jig.

Sing a song of sixpence, a pocket full of rye,
Four and twenty blackbirds baked in a pie.
When the pie was opened the birds began to sing,
And wasn't this a dainty dish to set before the king?
The king was in the parlor counting out his money;
The queen was in the kitchen eating bread and honey;
The maid was in the garden hanging out the clothes,
There came a little blackbird and nipped off her nose.

Three wise men of Gotham
Went to sea in a bowl.
  If the bowl had been stronger
  My song would be longer.

Little Miss Muffet
Sat on a tuffet
Eating some curds and whey.
There came a great spider,
That sat down beside her,
And frightened Miss Muffet away.

Georgy Porgy, pudding and pie,
Kissed the girls and made them cry.
When the boys came out to play,
Georgy Porgy ran away.

My Maid Mary she minds the dairy,
While I go a-hoeing and mowing each morn.
Gaily run the reel and the little spinning wheel,
While I am singing and mowing my corn.

This is the house that Jack built.

This is the malt
That lay in the house that Jack built.

This is the rat,
That ate the malt*
That lay in the house that Jack built.

This is the cat,
That killed the rat,
That ate the malt
That lay in the house that Jack built.

This is the dog,
That worried the cat,
That killed the rat,
That ate the malt
That lay in the house that Jack built.

This is the cow with the
    crumpled horn,
That tossed the dog,

That worried the cat,
That killed the rat,
That ate the malt
That lay in the house that Jack built.

This is the maiden all forlorn,
That milked the cow with the
    crumpled horn,
That tossed the dog,
That worried the cat,
That killed the rat,
That ate the malt
That lay in the house that Jack built.

This is the man all tattered and torn,
That kissed the maiden all forlorn,
That milked the cow with the
    crumpled horn,
That tossed the dog,
That worried the cat,
That killed the rat,
That ate the malt
That lay in the house that Jack built.

* malt—grain

This is the priest all
   shaven and shorn,
That married the man all
   tattered and torn,
That kissed the maiden all forlorn,
That milked the cow with the
   crumpled horn,
That tossed the dog,
That worried the cat,
That killed the rat,
That ate the malt
That lay in the house that Jack built.

This is the cock that crowed
   in the morn,
That waked the priest all
   shaven and shorn,
That married the man all
   tattered and torn,
That kissed the maiden all forlorn,
That milked the cow with the
   crumpled horn,

That tossed the dog,
That worried the cat,
That killed the rat,
That ate the malt
That lay in the house that Jack built.

This is the farmer sowing the corn,
That kept the cock that
   crowed in the morn,
That waked the priest all
   shaven and shorn,
That married the man all
   tattered and torn,
That kissed the maiden all forlorn,
That milked the cow with the
   crumpled horn,
That tossed the dog,
That worried the cat,
That killed the rat,
That ate the malt
That lay in the house that Jack built.

The boughs do shake and the bells do ring,
So merrily comes our harvest in,
Our harvest in, our harvest in,
So merrily comes our harvest in.

We've plowed, we've sowed,
We've reaped, we've mowed,
We've got our harvest in.

Dear, dear! What can the matter be?
Two old women got up in an apple tree.
One came down, and the other stayed till Saturday.

There were two birds sat upon a stone,
    Fal de ral-al de ral-laddy.
One flew away and then there was one.
    Fal de ral-al de ral-laddy.
The other flew after and then there was none.
    Fal de ral-al de ral-laddy.
So the poor stone was left all alone,
    Fal de ral-al de ral-laddy.
One of these little birds back again flew,
    Fal de ral-al de ral-laddy.
The other came after and then there were two,
    Fal de ral-al de ral-laddy.
Says one to the other: "Pray, how do you do?"
    Fal de ral-al de ral-laddy.
"Very well, thank you, and pray how are you?"
    Fal de ral-al de ral-laddy.

Tom, Tom, the piper's son,
Stole a pig, and away he run.
    The pig was eat,
    And Tom was beat,
And Tom ran crying down the street.

Little Polly Flinders
Sat among the cinders
　　Warming her pretty toes.
Her mother came and caught her,
Spanked her little daughter
　　For spoiling her nice new clothes.

Bye, Baby bunting,
Father's gone a-hunting,
Mother's gone a-milking,
Sister's gone a-silking,
And Brother's gone to buy a skin
To wrap the Baby bunting in.

Swan, swan, over the sea.
Swim, swan, swim!
Swan, swan, back again.
Well swum, swan!

 *This poem is a tongue-twister—it's very hard to say quickly. Try it and see.*

Bessy Bell and Mary Gray,
They were two bonny lasses.
They buid their house upon the lea,*
And covered it with rushes.

Bessy kept the garden gate,
And Mary kept the pantry.
Bessy always had to wait,
While Mary lived in plenty.

* lea—meadow

Old Sir Simon the king,
And young Sir Simon the squire,
And old Mrs. Hickabout
Kicked Mrs. Kickabout
Round about our coal fire.

If you are to be a gentleman,
And I suppose you'll be,
You'll neither laugh nor smile,
For a tickling of the knee.

Is your knee ticklish? Let's see!

Jack and Jill went up the hill
 To fetch a pail of water.
Jack fell down and broke his crown,
 And Jill came tumbling after.

Pussy cat, pussy cat, where have you been?
I've been to London to see the Queen.
Pussy cat, pussy cat, what did you there?
I frightened a little mouse under the chair.

Pat a cake, pat a cake, Baker's man;
Make me a cake as fast as you can.
Pat it and prick it and mark it with T,
Put it in the oven for Tommy and me.

*Can you do the hand motions
with me while we say this poem?*

Ring a ring o' roses,
A pocket full of posies.
Tisha! Tisha!
We all fall down.

As little Jenny Wren
Was sitting by her shed,
She waggled with her tail,
And nodded with her head.

She waggled with her tail,
And nodded with her head,
As little Jenny Wren
Was sitting by the shed.

Pussy-cat ate the dumplings, the dumplings,
Pussy-cat ate the dumplings.
Mamma stood by, and cried, "Oh fie!
Why did you eat the dumplings?"

There was a little woman, as I've been told,
Who was not very young, nor yet very old.
Now this little woman her living got
By selling codlins,* hot, hot, hot!

* codlins—apples

Little Boy Blue, come blow your horn,
The sheep's in the meadow, the cow's in the corn.
What! Is this the way you mind your sheep,
Under the haystack fast asleep?

The man in the moon came down too soon
  To inquire the way to Norridge.
The man in the south, he burnt his mouth
  With eating cold plum porridge.

Lucky Locket lost her pocket,*
Kitty Fisher found it.
There was not a penny in it,
But a ribbon round it.

* pocket—small, drawstring purse

There was an old woman tossed in a basket
   Seventeen times as high as the moon;
But where she was going no mortal could tell,
   For under her arm she carried a broom.

"Old woman, old woman, old woman," said I,
"Whither, oh whither, oh whither so high?"
"To sweep the cobwebs from the sky,
And I'll be with you by and by."

Dickery, dickery, dare,
The pig flew up in the air.
The man in brown soon brought him down,
Dickery, dickery, dare.

Hannah Bantry,
In the pantry,
Gnawing at a mutton bone.
How she gnawed it,
How she clawed it,
When she found herself alone.

Round and round the rugged rock
The ragged rascal ran.
How many R's are there in that?
Now tell me if you can.

How many R's did you hear?

A well
As round as an apple, as deep as a cup,
And all the king's horses can't pull it up.

Cold and raw the north winds blow
Bleak in the morning early.
All the hills are covered with snow,
And winter's now come fairly.

What are some fun things to do in the snow?

"To bed, to bed," says Sleepy-Head.
"Let's stay awhile," says Slow.
"Put on the pot," says Greedy Sot.
"We'll sup before we go."

Diddle, diddle, dumpling, my son John,
Went to bed with his breeches on,
One stocking off, and one stocking on,
Diddle, diddle, dumpling, my son John.

Little Tom Tucker
Sings for his supper.
What shall he eat?
White bread and butter.
How will he cut it
Without e'er a knife?
How will he marry
Without e'er a wife?

Here we go round the mulberry bush,
The mulberry bush, the mulberry bush,
Here we go round the mulberry bush,
On a cold and frosty morning.

This is the way we wash our hands,
Wash our hands, wash our hands,
This is the way we wash our hands,
On a cold and frosty morning.

This is the way we wash our clothes,
Wash our clothes, wash our clothes,
This is the way we wash our clothes,
On a cold and frosty morning.

This is the way we go to school,
Go to school, go to school,
This is the way we go to school,
On a cold and frosty morning.

This is the way we come out of school,
Come out of school, come out of school,
This is the way we come out of school,
On a cold and frosty morning.

 *What are some of the fun things to do in school?*

Humpty Dumpty sat on a wall,
Humpty Dumpty had a great fall.
All the king's horses and all the king's men
Couldn't put Humpty together again.

High diddle diddle,
The cat and the fiddle,
The cow jumped over the moon.
The little dog laughed
To see such craft,
And the dish ran away with the spoon.

When I was a little boy I lived by myself,
And all the bread and cheese I got I put upon a shelf.
The rats and the mice, they made such a strife,
I was forced to go to London to buy me a wife.
The streets were so broad and the lanes were so narrow,
I was forced to bring my wife home in a wheelbarrow.
The wheelbarrow broke and my wife had a fall,
And down came the wheelbarrow, wife and all.

Robin and Richard
  Were two sleepyheads.
They spend the day
  Just lazing in bed.
Then up starts Robin
  And looks at the sky:
"Oh, brother Richard,
  The sun's very high.
You go before
  With the bottle and bag,
And I will come after
  On little Jack nag."

Are you a sleepyhead?

'Twas once upon a time, when Jenny Wren was young,
So daintily she danced and so prettily she sung,
Robin Redbreast lost his heart, for he was a gallant bird,
So he doffed his hat to Jenny Wren, requesting to be heard.

"O, dearest Jenny Wren, if you will but be mine,
You shall feed on cherry pie and drink new currant wine,
I'll dress you like a goldfinch or any peacock gay.
So, dearest Jen, if you'll be mine let us appoint the day."

Jenny blushed behind her fan and thus declared her mind:
"Since, dearest Bob, I love you well, I take your offer kind;
Cherry pie is very nice and so is currant wine,
But I must wear my plain brown gown and never go too fine."

You shall have an apple,
You shall have a plum,
You shall have a rattle,
When papa comes home.

When I was a little girl,
About seven years old,
I hadn't got a petticoat,
To cover me from the cold.

So I went into Darlington,
That pretty little town,
And there I bought a petticoat,
A cloak, and a gown.

I went into the woods
And built me a kirk.*
And all the birds of the air,
They helped me to work.

The hawk with his long claws
Pulled down the stone,
The dove with her rough bill
Brought me them home.

The parrot was the clergyman,
The peacock was the clerk,
The bullfinch played the organ,
We made merry work.

*kirk—church

Donkey, donkey, old and gray,
Open your mouth and gently bray.
Lift your ears and blow your horn,
To wake the world this sleepy morn.

Can you make a sound like a donkey?

If all the world were apple pie,
And all the sea were ink,
And all the trees were bread and cheese,
What should we have to drink?

I had a little hen, the prettiest ever seen.
She washed me the dishes and kept the house clean.
She went to the mill to fetch me some flour,
And always got home in less than an hour.
She baked me my bread, she brewed me my ale,
She sat by the fire and told many a fine tale.

Is John Smith within?—Yes, that he is.
Can he set a shoe? Ay, marry, two.
Here a nail and there a nail.
Tick-tack-too.

Did you know that horses wore shoes?

Little King Boggen he built a fine hall,
Pie-crust and pasty-crust, that was the wall;
The windows were made of black puddings and white,
And slated* with pancakes—you ne'er saw the like!

*slated—roof-tiled

How many days has my baby to play?
Saturday, Sunday, Monday,
Tuesday, Wednesday, Thursday, Friday,
Saturday, Sunday, Monday.

Little Jack Horner
Sat in a corner
Eating a Christmas pie.
He put in his thumb,
And pulled out a plum,
And said: "Oh, what a good boy am I!"

On Saturday night I lost my wife,
And where do you think I found her?
Up in the moon, singing a tune,
And all the stars around her.

Rain, rain, go away,
Come again another day;
Little Johnny wants to play.

*Now say this poem
with your name.*

As I went to Bonner
    I met a pig
    Without a wig,
Upon my word and honor.

Do pigs wear wigs?

The Queen of Hearts,
She made some tarts
All on a summer's day.
The Knave of Hearts,
He stole those tarts,
And took them clean away.

The King of Hearts
Called for the tarts,
And beat the Knave full sore.
The Knave of Hearts
Brought back the tarts,
And vowed he'd steal no more.

Goosey, goosey, gander, where dost thou wander?
"Upstairs and downstairs and in my lady's chamber.
There I met an old man that wouldn't say his prayers,
I took him by his hind legs and threw him downstairs."

See saw, Margery Daw,
    Jacky shall have a new master:
Jacky must have but a penny a day
    Because he can work no faster.

A was an archer, who shot at a frog.

B was a butcher, and had a great dog.

C was a captain, all covered with lace.

D was a duncehead, and had a red face.

E was an esquire, with pride on his brow.

F was a farmer, and followed the plow.

G was a gamester, who had but ill-luck.

H was a hunter, and hunted a buck.

I was an innkeeper, who loved to carouse.

J was a joiner, and built up a house.

K was King William, once governed
this land.

L was a lady, who had a white hand.

M was a miser, and hoarded up gold.

N was a nobleman, gallant and bold.

O was an oyster girl, and went about town.

P was a parson, and wore a black gown.

Q was a queen, who wore a silk slip.

R was a robber, and wanted a whip.

S was a sailor, and spent all he got.

T was a tinker, and mended a pot.

U was a usurer,* a miserable elf.

V was a vintner, who drank all himself.

W was a watchman, and guarded the door.

X was expensive, and so became poor.

Y was a youth, that did not love school.

Z was a zany, a poor harmless fool.

*usurer—money lender

Darby and Joan were dressed in black,
Sword and buckle behind their back.
Foot for foot, and knee for knee,
Turn about Darby's company.

Solomon Grundy,
Born on Monday,
Christened on Tuesday,
Married on Wednesday,
Took ill on Thursday,
Worse on Friday,
Died on Saturday,
Buried on Sunday.
This is the end
Of Solomon Grundy.

Daffy-down-dilly is now come to town
With a petticoat green and bright yellow gown.

Can you guess what Daffy-down-dilly is?

The lion and the unicorn
  Were fighting for the crown.
The lion beat the unicorn
  All about the town.
Some gave them white bread,
  And some gave them brown:
Some gave them plum-cake,
  And sent them out of town.

Old King Cole
Was a merry old soul,
And a merry old soul was he.
He called for his pipe,
And he called for his bowl,
And he called for his fiddlers three.

This little piggy went to market,
That little piggy stayed home;
This little piggy had roast beef,
That little piggy had none;
This little piggy went,
"Wee, wee, wee!"
All the way home.

What is the sound a pig makes?
What is the sound a cow makes?
How about a cat? A dog?

Cackle, cackle, Mother Goose,
Have you any feathers loose?
Truly have I, pretty fellow,
Half enough to fill a pillow.
Here are quills, take one or two,
And down to make a bed for you.

In marble walls as white as milk,
Lined with a skin as soft as silk,
Within a fountain crystal-clear,
A golden apple doth appear.
No doors there are to this stronghold,
Yet thieves break in and steal the gold.

Bonny lass, pretty lass,
  Wilt thou be mine?
Thou shalt not wash dishes
  Nor yet serve the swine.
Thou shalt sit on a cushion
  And sew a fine seam,
And thou shalt eat strawberries,
  Sugar and cream.

Mistress Mary, quite contrary
How does your garden grow?
With silver bells and cockleshells
And pretty maids all in a row.

Handy-spandy, Jacky dandy,
Loves plum cake and sugar candy.
He bought some at a grocer's shop,
And please away went hop, hop, hop.

Ding—dong—bell, the cat's in the well.
Who put her in? Little Johnny Green.
Who pulled her out? Great Johnny Stout.
What a naughty boy was that
To drown poor pussy cat,
Who never did him any harm,
And killed the mice in his father's barn.

Old Mother Hubbard
Went to the cupboard
    To get her poor dog a bone.
But when she came there
The cupboard was bare,
    And so the poor dog had none.

Red stockings, blue stockings,
Shoes tied up with silver.
A red rosette upon my breast
And a gold ring on my finger.

Doctor Foster went to Gloucester
In a shower of rain.
He stepped in a puddle,
Right up to his middle,
And never went there again.

Elsie Marley is grown so fine,
She won't get up to feed the swine,
But lies in bed till eight or nine.
Lazy Elsie Marley.

One, two—-buckle my shoe.
Three, four—knock at the door.
Five, six—pick up sticks.
Seven, eight—lay them straight.
Nine, ten—a good fat hen.
Eleven, twelve—dig and delve.
Thirteen, fourteen—maids a-courting.
Fifteen, sixteen— maids in the kitchen;
Seventeen, eighteen—maids in waiting;
Nineteen, twenty—my plate's empty.

Let's make a rhyme!
Finish these:
One, two _____
Three, four _____
Five, six _____
Seven, eight _____
Nine, ten _____

There were two blackbirds sitting on a hill,
One named Jack and other named Jill.
Fly away, Jack! Fly away, Jill!
Come again, Jack! Come again, Jill!

Polly, put the kettle on,
Polly, put the kettle on,
Polly, put the kettle on,
  We'll all have tea.
Sukey, take it off again,
Sukey, take it off again,
Sukey, take it off again,
  They're all gone away.

Peas-porridge hot,
  Peas-porridge cold,
Peas-porridge in the pot
  Nine days old.
Spell me that in four letters:
  I will: T H A T.

The sow came in with the saddle,
The little pig rocked the cradle,
The dish jumped up on the table
To see the pot swallow the ladle.
The spit* that stood behind the door
Threw the pudding-stick on the floor.
"Odsplut!" said the gridiron,
    "Can't you agree?
I'm the head constable,
    Bring them to me!"

*spit—roasting rod

Cross patch, draw the latch,
  Sit by the fire and spin.
Take a cup and drink it up,
  Then call your neighbors in.

A swarm of bees in May
Is worth a load of hay.
A swarm of bees in June
Is worth a silver spoon.
A swarm of bees in July
Is not worth a fly.

Down by the river
Where the green grass grows
Pretty Polly Perkins
Bleaches her clothes.
She laughs and she sings,
And she sings so sweet.
She calls, Come over,
Across the street.
He kissed her, he kissed her,
He took her to town;
He bought her a ring
And a damascene* gown.

*damascene—patterned

My little old man and I fell out.
I'll tell you 'twas all about:
I had money and he had none,
And that's the way the noise begun.

There was an old woman
  Sold puddings and pies;
She went to the mill,
  And dust flew in her eyes.
While through the streets,
To all she meets
  She ever cries:
  "Hot pies—hot pies."

A farmer went trotting upon his gray mare,
  Bumpety, bumpety, bump,
With his daughter behind him, so rosy and fair,
  Lumpety, lumpety, lump.

A raven cried "Croak," and they all tumbled down,
  Bumpety, bumpety, bump;
The mare broke her knees and the farmer his crown,
  Lumpety, lumpety, lump.

The mischievous raven flew laughing away,
  Bumpety, bumpety, bump,
And vowed he would serve them the same next day,
  Lumpety, lumpety, lump.

"Old woman, old woman, shall we go a-shearing?"
"Speak a little louder, sir, I'm very thick o' hearing."
"Old woman, old woman, shall I kiss you dearly?"
"Thank you, kind sir, I hear very clearly."

Betty Botter bought some butter,
But she said, the butter's bitter;
If I put it in my batter
It will make my batter bitter,
But a bit of better butter,
That would make my batter better.
So she bought a bit of butter
Better than her bitter butter,
And she put it in her batter
And the batter was not bitter.
So 'twas better Betty Botter
Bought a bit of better butter.

*What are some other
words that start with B?*

Mrs. Mason bought a basin,
Mrs. Tyson said, What a nice 'un.
What did it cost? Said Mrs. Frost.
Half a crown, said Mrs. Brown.
Did it indeed, said Mrs. Reed.
It did for certain, said Mrs. Burton.
Then Mrs. Nix up to her tricks
Threw the basin on the bricks.

She sells sea-shells on the sea shore;
The shells that she sells are sea-shells I'm sure.
So if she sells sea-shells on the sea shore,
I'm sure that the shells are sea-shore shells.

Jeremiah Obadiah, puff, puff, puff.
When he gives his messages, he snuffs, snuffs, snuffs,
When he goes to school by day, he roars, roars, roars,
When he goes to bed at night, he snores, snores, snores,
When he goes to Christmas treat, he eats plum-duff,
Jeremiah Obadiah, puff, puff, puff.

As I was going to St. Ives
I met a man with seven wives.
Every wife had seven sacks.
Every sack had seven cats.
Every cat had seven kits.
Kits, cats, sacks and wives,
How many were going to St. Ives?*

* No man, no kits, no cats, no sacks, no
wives—only "I" was going to St. Ives

There was an old woman, and what do you think?
She lived upon nothing but vittles and drink;
Vittles and drink were the chief of her diet,
And yet this old woman could never be quiet.

Jack Sprat could eat no fat.
  His wife could eat no lean;
So 'twixt them both they cleared the cloth,
  And licked the platter clean.

I saw a fishpond all on fire.
I saw a house bow to a squire.
I saw a parson twelve feet high.
I saw a cottage near the sky.
I saw a balloon made of lead.
I saw a coffin drop down dead.
I saw two sparrows run a race.
I saw two horses making lace.
I saw a girl just like a cat.
I saw a kitten wear a hat.
I saw a man who saw these, too,
And said, though strange,
      they were all true.

Let's make up some strange things to see.

There was a piper had a cow,
And he had naught to give her.
He pulled out his pipes and played her a tune,
And bade the cow consider.

The cow considered very well,
And gave the piper a penny,
And bade him play the other tune,
"Corn rigs are bonny."*

*an old Scottish song
by Robert Burns

There was a crooked man,
  And he went a crooked mile,
He found a crooked sixpence
  Beside a crooked stile.*
He bought a crooked cat
  Which caught a crooked mouse,
And they all lived together
  In a little crooked house.

*stile—steps over a wall or fence

I had a little husband no bigger than my thumb,
I put him in a pint pot, and there I bid him drum.
I bought a little handkerchief to wipe his little nose,
And a pair of little garters to tie his little hose.

Great A, little a,
Bouncing B.
The cat's in the cupboard,
And she can't see.

The man in the wilderness
  Asked me
How many strawberries
  Grew in the sea.
I answered him
  As I thought good,
As many red herrings
  As grew in the wood.

Little Bobby Snooks was fond of his books,
And loved by his usher and master.
But naughty Jack Spry, he got a black eye,
And carries his nose in a plaster.*

Friday night's dream, on Saturday told,
Is sure to come true, be it never so old.

Barber, barber, shave a pig.
How many hairs will make a wig?
Four and twenty; that's enough.
Give the barber a pinch of snuff.

*plaster—a sticky paste to cover a wound

As I was going along, along,
A-singing a comical song, song, song,
The lane that I went was so long, long, long,
And the song that I sang was so long, long, long,
And so I went singing along.

This is the way the ladies ride,
Prim, prim, prim.
This is the way the gentlemen ride,
Trim, trim, trim.
Presently come the country folks,
Hobbledy gee, hobbledy gee.

"Jacky, come give me your fiddle,
  If ever you mean to thrive."
"Nay, I'll not give my fiddle
  To any man alive.

"If I should give my fiddle
  They'll think that I'm gone mad,
For many a joyful day
  My fiddle and I have had."

Have you ever heard someone play a fiddle? What's another name for a fiddle?

When good King Arthur ruled his land
  He was a goodly king.
But he stole three pecks of barley meal
  To make a bag-pudding.
A bag-pudding the king did make,
  And stuffed it well with plums,
And in it put great lumps of fat
  As big as my two thumbs.
The king and queen did eat thereof,
  And noblemen beside,
And what they could not eat that night
  The queen next morning fried.

Hark! Hark!
The dogs do bark,
The beggars are coming to town.
Some in rags,
Some in tags,
And some in velvet gowns.

As I was going up Primrose Hill,
 Primrose Hill was dirty.
There I met a pretty lass,
 And she dropped me a curtsey.

Little lass, pretty lass,
 Blessings light upon you;
If I had half-a-crown a day,
 I'd spend it all upon you.

Bat, bat,
Come under my hat,
And I'll give you a slice of bacon.
And when I bake
I'll give you a cake,
If I am not mistaken.

Christmas is coming,
    the goose is getting fat.
Please put a penny
    in the old man's hat.
If you haven't got a penny
    a ha'penny will do,
If you haven't got a ha'penny,
    God bless you.

> *What do you think*
> *a ha'penny is?*

Christmas comes but once a year,
And when it comes it brings good cheer.

One, two, three, four, five,
I caught a hare alive.
Six, seven, eight, nine, ten,
I let him go again.

Can you count backward from ten?

The north wind doth blow,
And we shall have snow,
And what will poor robin do then?
Poor thing!

He'll sit in the barn
And keep himself warm,
And hide his head under his wing.
Poor thing!

There was a little boy went into a barn
  And lay down on some hay.
A calf came out and smelled about,
  And the little boy ran away.

"You owe me five shillings,"
Say the bells of St. Helen's.

"When will you pay me?"
Say the bells of Old Bailey.

"When I grow rich,"
Say the bells of Shoreditch.

"When will that be?"
Say the bells of Stepney.

"I do not know,"
Says the great Bell of Bow.

"Two sticks in an apple,"
Ring the bells of Whitechapel.

"Halfpence and farthings,"
Say the bells of St. Martin's.

"Kettles and pans,"
Say the bells of St. Ann's.

"Brickbats and tiles,"
Say the bells of St. Giles.

"Old shoes and slippers,"
Say the bells of St. Peter's.

"Pokers and tongs,"
Say the bells of St. John's.

Play along with your fingers as we read this rhyme.

Dance, Thumbkin, dance,
  (Keep the thumb in motion)
Dance, ye merry men, everyone.
  (All the fingers in motion)
For Thumbkin, he can dance alone,
  (The thumb moving alone)
Thumbkin, he can dance alone.
  (The thumb moving alone)
Dance, Foreman, dance,
  (The first finger moving)
Dance, ye merry men, everyone.
  (All moving)
But Foreman, he can dance alone,
  (The first finger moving)
Foreman, he can dance alone.
  (The first finger moving)
Dance, Longman, dance,
  (The middle, longest finger
  moving)
Dance, ye merry men, everyone.
  (All moving)

For Longman, he can dance alone,
  (The middle, longest finger
  moving)
Longman, he can dance alone.
  (The middle, longest finger
  moving)
Dance, Ringman, dance,
  (The ring finger moving)
Dance, ye merry men, dance.
  (All moving)
But Ringman cannot dance alone,
  (The ring finger moving)
Ringman, he cannot dance alone.
  (The ring finger moving)
Dance, Littleman, dance,
  (The pinky moving)
Dance, ye merry men, dance.
  (All moving)
But Littleman, he can dance alone,
  (The pinky moving)
Littleman, he can dance alone.
  (The pinky moving)

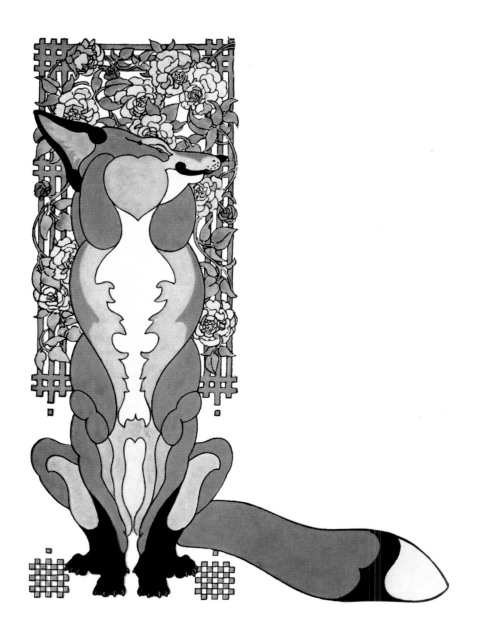

FOLK TALES

The LITTLE RED HEN

One day as the Little Red Hen was scratching in a field, she found a grain of wheat.

"This wheat should be planted," she said. "Who will plant this grain of wheat?"

Can you see the gain of wheat in the picture?

"Not I," said the Duck.

"Not I," said the Cat.

"Not I," said the Dog.

"Then I will," said Little Red Hen. And she did.

Soon the wheat grew to be tall and yellow.

"The wheat is ripe," said the Little Red Hen. "Who will cut the wheat?"

"Not I," said the Duck.

"Not I," said the Cat.

"Not I," said the Dog.

"Then I will," said the Little Red Hen. And she did.

When the wheat was cut, the Little Red Hen said, "Who will thresh this wheat?"

"Not I," said the Duck.

"Not I," said the Cat.

"Not I," said the Dog.

"Then I will," said the Little Red Hen. And she did.

When the wheat was all threshed, the Little Red Hen said, "Who will take this wheat to the mill?"

"Not I," said the Duck.

"Not I," said the Cat.

"Not I," said the Dog.

"Then I will," said the Little Red Hen. And she did.

She took the wheat to the mill and had it ground into flour. Then she said, "Who will make this flour into bread?"

"Not I," said the Duck.

"Not I," said the Cat.

"Not I," said the Dog.

"Then I will," said the Little Red Hen. And she did.

She made and baked the bread. Then she said, "Who will eat this bread?"

"Oh! I will," said the Duck.

"And I will," said the Cat.

"And I will," said the Dog.

 *Do you think that the Duck, the Dog and the Cat deserve to eat the bread? Why?*

"No, no!" said the Little Red Hen. "I will do that." And she did.

The OLD WOMAN AND HER PIG

Once, an old woman found a crooked sixpence while sweeping her doorway. "What shall I do with this sixpence?" she said. "I will go to the market and buy a pig."

So the old woman went to the market and bought a pig.

On her way home, she came to a stile.* But the pig would not climb over it.

*stile—steps over a wall or fence.

"Pig, pig, get over the stile,
Or I cannot get home tonight."

But the pig would not.
She went a little farther and met a dog, and she said to the dog:

"Dog, dog, bite pig.
Pig won't get over the stile,
And I cannot get home tonight."

But the dog would not.

She went a little farther and met a stick, and she said to the stick:

"Stick, stick, beat dog.
Dog won't bite pig,
Pig won't get over the stile,
And I cannot get home tonight."

But the stick would not.

She went a little farther and met a fire, and she said to the fire:

"Fire, fire, burn stick.
Stick won't beat dog,
Dog won't bite pig,
Pig won't get over the stile,
And I cannot get home tonight."

But the fire would not.

She went a little farther and met some water, and she said to the water:

"Water, water, quench fire.
Fire won't burn stick,
Stick won't beat dog,
Dog won't bite pig,
Pig won't get over the stile,
And I cannot get home tonight."

But the water would not.

She went a little farther and met an ox, and she said to the ox:

"Ox, ox, drink water.
Water won't quench fire,
Fire won't burn stick,
Stick won't beat dog,
Dog won't bite pig,
Pig won't get over the stile,
And I cannot get home tonight."

But the ox would not.

She went a little farther and met a butcher, and she said to the butcher:

"Butcher, butcher, pen ox.
Ox won't drink water,
Water won't quench fire,
Fire won't burn stick,
Stick won't beat dog,
Dog won't bite pig,
Pig won't get over the stile,
And I cannot get home tonight."

How would you try to get the pig home?

But the butcher would not.

She went a little farther and met a rope, and she said to the rope:

"Rope, rope, whip butcher.
Butcher won't pen ox,
Ox won't drink water,
Water won't quench fire,
Fire won't burn stick,
Stick won't beat dog,
Dog won't bite pig,
Pig won't get over the stile,
And I cannot get home tonight."

But the rope would not.

She went a little farther and met a rat, and she said to the rat:

"Rat, rat, gnaw rope.
Rope won't whip butcher,
Butcher won't pen ox,
Ox won't drink water,
Water won't quench fire,
Fire won't burn stick,

Stick won't beat dog,
Dog won't bite pig,
Pig won't get over the stile,
And I cannot get home tonight."

But the rat would not.

She went a little farther and met a cat, and she said to the cat:

"Cat, cat, bite rat.
Rat won't gnaw rope,
Rope won't whip butcher,
Butcher won't pen ox,
Ox won't drink water,
Water won't quench fire,
Fire won't burn stick,
Stick won't beat dog,
Dog won't bite pig,
And I cannot get
    home tonight."

The cat said to her, "If you will get me a saucer of milk, I will bite the rat."

So the old woman gave a wisp of hay to a cow that was near, and the cow gave her a saucer of milk. The old woman gave the saucer of milk to the cat.

And this is what happened:

The cat began to bite the rat; the rat began to gnaw the rope; the rope began to whip the butcher; the butcher began to pen the ox; the ox began to drink the water; the water began to quench the fire; the fire began to burn the stick; the stick began to beat the dog; the dog began to bite the pig; and the pig got over the stile.

And the old woman *did* get home that night.

CHICKEN LICKEN

One day, when Chicken Licken was scratching among leaves, an acorn fell out of a tree and struck her on the tail.

"Oh," said Chicken Licken. "The sky is falling! I am going to tell the King."

So she went along and went along until she met Henny Penny.

"Good morning, Chicken Licken. Where are you going?" asked Henny Penny.

"Oh, Henny Penny, the sky is falling, and I am going to tell the King!"

"How do you know the sky is falling?" asked Henny Penny.

"I saw it with my own eyes, I heard it with my own ears, and a piece of it fell on my tail!" said Chicken Licken.

"Then I will go with you," said Henny Penny.

So they went along and went along until they met Cocky Locky.

"Good morning, Henny Penny and Chicken Licken," said Cocky Locky. "Where are you going?"

"Oh, Cocky Locky, the sky is falling, and we are going to tell the King!"

"How do you know the sky is falling?" asked Cocky Locky.

"Chicken Licken told me," said Henny Penny.

"I saw it with my own eyes, I heard it with my own ears, and a piece of it fell on my tail!" said Chicken Licken.

"Then I will go with you," said Cocky Locky, "and we will tell the King."

So they went along and went along until they met Ducky Daddles. "Good morning, Cocky Locky, Henny Penny, and Chicken Licken," said Ducky Daddles. "Where are you going?"

"Oh, Ducky Daddles, the sky is falling, and we are going to tell the King."

"How do you know the sky is falling?" asked Ducky Daddles.

"Henny Penny told me," said Cocky Locky.

"Chicken Licken told me," said Henny Penny.

"I saw it with my own eyes, I heard it with my own ears, and a piece of it fell on my tail!" said Chicken Licken.

"Then I will go with you," said Ducky Daddles, "and we will tell the King."

So they went along and went along until they met Goosey Loosey.

"Good morning, Ducky Daddles, Cocky Locky, Henny Penny, and Chicken Licken," said Goosey Loosey. "Where are you going?"

"Oh, Goosey Loosey, the sky is falling, and we are going to tell the King."

"How do you know the sky is falling?" asked Goosey Loosey.

"Cocky Locky told me," said Ducky Daddles.

"Henny Penny told me," said Cocky Locky.

"Chicken Licken told me," said Henny Penny.

"I saw it with my own eyes, I heard it with my own ears, and a piece of it fell on my tail!" said Chicken Licken.

"Then I will go with you," said Goosey Loosey, "and we will tell the King."

So they went along and went along until they met Turkey Lurkey.

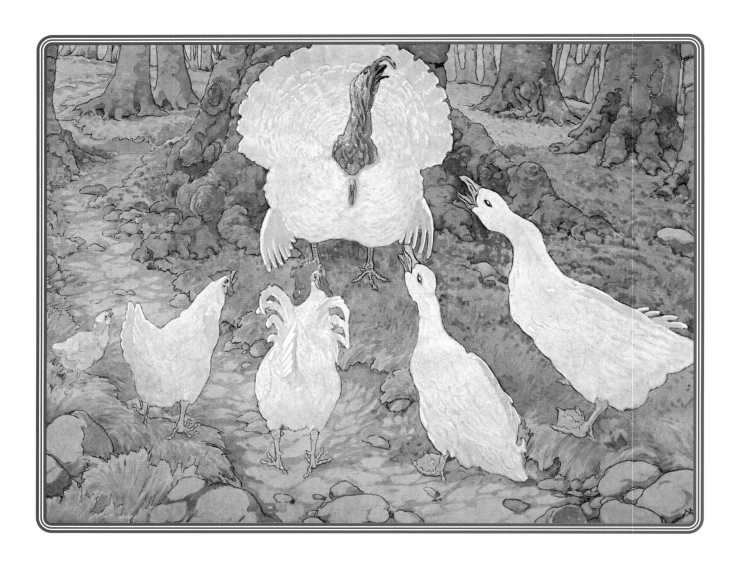

"Good morning, Goosey Loosey, Ducky Daddles, Cocky Locky, Henny Penny, and Chicken Licken," said Turkey Lurkey. "Where are you going?"

"Oh, Turkey Lurkey, the sky is falling, and we are going to tell the King!"

"How do you know the sky is falling?" asked Turkey Lurkey.

"Ducky Daddles told me," said Goosey Loosey.

"Cocky Locky told me," said Ducky Daddles.

"Henny Penny told me," said Cocky Locky.

"Chicken Licken told me," said Henny Penny.

"I saw it with my own eyes, I heard it with my own ears, and a piece of it fell on my tail!" said Chicken Licken.

"Then I will go with you," said Turkey Lurkey, "and we will tell the King!"

So they all went along and went along until they met Foxy Woxy.

"Good morning, Turkey Lurkey, Goosey Loosey, Ducky Daddles, Cocky Locky, Henny Penny and Chicken Licken," said Foxy Woxy. "Where are you going?"

"Oh, Foxy Woxy, the sky is falling, and we are going to tell the King!"

"How do you know the sky is falling?" asked Foxy Woxy.

"Goosey Loosey told me," said Turkey Lurkey.

"Ducky Daddles told me," said Goosey Loosey.

"Cocky Locky told me," said Ducky Daddles.

"Henny Penny told me," said Cocky Locky.

"Chicken Licken told me," said Henny Penny.

"I saw it with my own eyes, I heard it with my own ears, and a piece of it fell on my tail!" said Chicken Licken.

Do you think Foxy Woxy believes the sky is falling? What do you think he's thinking?

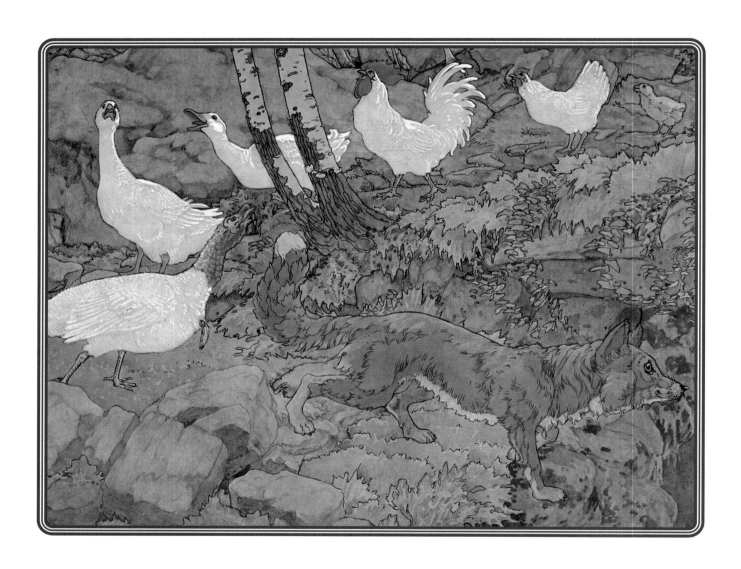

"Then we will run, we will run to my den," said Foxy Woxy, "and I will tell the King."

And the King was never told that the sky was falling.

Why do you think the King was never told the sky was falling?

THE THREE BILLY GOATS GRUFF

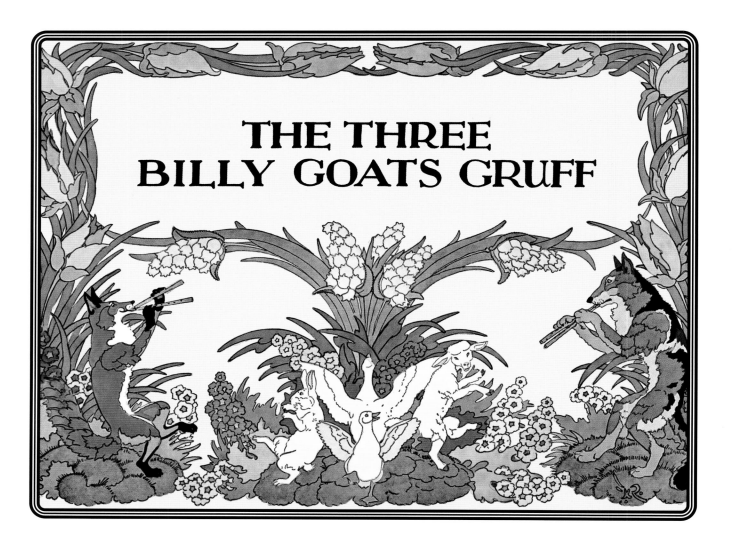

Once upon a time there were three billy goats, who wanted to go up to the hillside to make themselves fat, and the name of all three was Gruff.

On the way up was a bridge over a burn* they had to cross. Under the bridge lived a great ugly Troll, with eyes as big as saucers, and a nose as long as a poker.

So first of all came the youngest billy goat Gruff to cross the bridge.

"Trip, trap, trip, trap!" went the bridge.

"WHO'S THAT tripping over my bridge?" roared the Troll.

"Oh! It is only I, the tiniest billy goat Gruff; and I'm going up to the hillside to make myself fat," said the billy goat with such a small voice.

"Now, I'm coming to gobble you up," said the Troll.

*burn—small stream or brook

"Oh, no! Pray don't take me. I'm too little, that I am," said the billy goat. "Wait a bit till the second billy goat Gruff comes. He's much bigger."

"Well! Be off with you," said the Troll.

A little while after came the second billy goat Gruff to cross the bridge.

"TRIP, TRAP! TRIP, TRAP! TRIP, TRAP!" went the bridge,

"WHO'S THAT tripping over my bridge?" roared the Troll.

"Oh! It's the second billy goat Gruff, and I'm going up to the hillside to make myself fat," said the billy goat, who hadn't such a small voice.

The Troll certainly is an odd-looking fellow. How would you describe him?

"Now, I'm coming to gobble you up," said the Troll.

"Oh, no! Don't take me. Wait a little till the big billy goat Gruff comes. He's much bigger."

"Very well! Be off with you," said the Troll.

But just then up came the big billy goat Gruff.

"TRIP, TRAP! TRIP, TRAP! TRIP, TRAP!" went the bridge, for the billy goat was so heavy that the bridge creaked and groaned under him.

"WHO'S THAT tramping over my bridge?" roared the Troll.

"IT'S I! THE BIG BILLY GOAT GRUFF," said the billy goat, who had an ugly, hoarse voice of his own.

"Now, I'm coming to gobble you up," roared the Troll.

"Well, come along! I've got two spears,
And I'll poke your nose and pierce your ears;
I've got besides two curling-stones,*
And I'll bruise your body and rattle your bones."

That was what the big billy goat said. And he flew at the Troll, and tossed him out into the burn, and after that he went up to the hillside.

*curling-stones—heavy stones used in the ice-sport called Curling. In this case, he means his big, heavy hooves.

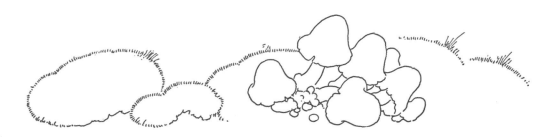

There the billy goats got so fat they were scarcely able to walk home again; and if the fat hasn't fallen off them— why, they're still fat. And so:

Snip, snap, snout
This tale's told out.

LITTLE TUPPENS

Long, long ago an old hen and her one little chicken
went into the woods. The little chicken was named
Tuppens. *Scratch, scratch*, they were busy all day among
the leaves finding seeds to eat.

"Do not eat the big seeds," said the old hen to Little
Tuppens, "for they will make you cough."

But by and by Little Tuppens found a big seed and ate it.
Then Little Tuppens began to cough. The old hen was
frightened at this and ran to the spring.

She said:

"Please, spring, give me some water.
Little Tuppens is coughing."

The spring said:

"Get me a cup and then I will give you some water."

The old hen ran to the oak tree and said:

"Please, oak tree, give me a cup;
Then the spring will give me some water.
Little Tuppens is coughing."

The oak tree said:

"Shake me. Then I will give you a cup."

The old hen ran to a little boy and said:

"Please, little boy, shake the oak tree;
Then the oak tree will give me a cup,
And the spring will give me some water.
Little Tuppens is coughing."

The little boy said:

"Give me some shoes. Then I can shake
  the oak tree for you."

The old hen ran to the shoemaker and said:

"Please, good shoemaker,
  give me some shoes for the little boy;
Then the little boy will shake the oak tree,
And the oak tree will give me a cup,
And the spring will give me some water.
Little Tuppens is coughing."

The shoemaker said:

"Get me some leather and then
I will make some shoes for the little boy."

The old hen ran to the cow and said:

"Please, cow, give me some leather;
  Then the shoemaker will make
    shoes for the little boy,
  And the little boy will shake the oak tree,
  And the oak tree will give me a cup,
  And the spring will give me some water.
  Little Tuppens is coughing."

The cow said:

"Get me some corn and then
I will give you some leather."

The old hen ran to the farmer and said:

"Please, farmer, give me corn for the cow;
Then the cow will give me some
    leather for the shoemaker,
And the shoemaker will make
    shoes for the little boy,
    And the little boy will shake the oak tree,
    And the oak tree will give me a cup,
    And the spring will give me some water.
Little Tuppens is coughing."

The farmer said:

"Get me a plow and then I can
    give you some corn."

The old hen ran to the blacksmith and said:

"Please, good blacksmith, give me a plow for the farmer;
Then the farmer will give me some
  corn for the cow,
And the cow will give me some
  leather for the shoemaker,
And the shoemaker will give me
  some shoes for the little boy,
And the little boy will shake the oak tree,
And the oak tree will give me a cup,
And the spring will give me some water.
Little Tuppens is coughing."

The blacksmith said:

"Get me some iron and then I can give you
  a plow."

The old hen ran to the dwarfs and asked for iron for the blacksmith. When she had told her story about Little Tuppens to the dwarfs, they wanted to help. They went into their cave and brought out some iron for the blacksmith.

Then the blacksmith made a plow for the farmer,
And the farmer gave some corn for the cow,
And the cow gave some leather for the shoemaker,
And the shoemaker made
    some shoes for the little boy,
And the little boy shook
    the oak tree,
And the oak tree gave a cup,
And the spring gave some
    water,
And the old hen gave the
    water to Little Tuppens,

And Little Tuppens
    stopped coughing.

*When you help other
people, it makes a
difference, doesn't it?
Can you tell me about
times you've been helpful?*

THE STRAW OX

Once upon a time, there was an old man and an old woman. The old man worked in the fields, while the old woman sat at home and spun flax. They were so poor that they could save nothing at all. All their earnings they spent on food, and when that was gone, there was nothing left.

At last the old woman had a good idea.

"Look, now, husband," she said, "make me a straw ox, and smear it all over with tar."

"Why, you foolish woman!" said he. "What's the good of such an ox?"

"Never mind," said she, "you just make it. I know what I am about."

What was the poor man to do?

He set to work and made the ox of straw, and smeared it all over with tar.

The night passed away, and at early dawn the old woman took her staff and drove the straw ox out to graze. She herself sat down behind a hill and began spinning her flax, crying, "Graze away, little ox, while I spin my flax!"

As she spun, her head drooped down and she began to doze. And while she was dozing, out from the dark woods a bear came rushing upon the ox and said, "Who are you? Speak and tell me!"

"A three-year-old heifer am I," said the ox, "made of straw and smeared with tar."

"Oh!" said the bear. "Stuffed with straw and trimmed with tar, are you? Then give me some straw and tar, so I may patch up my ragged fur!"

"Take some," said the ox.

The bear fell upon the ox and tried to tear away the tar. He tore and tore and buried his teeth in it. But he found he couldn't let go. He tugged and he tugged, but it was no good, and the ox dragged him off—goodness knows where.

When the old woman awoke, there was no ox to be seen. "Alas! Old fool that I am!" she cried. "Perchance it has gone home."

She quickly caught up her staff and spinning-board, threw them over her shoulders, and hastened off home. And there was the ox. It had dragged the bear up to the fence. So she went in and called her husband. "Look! Look!" she cried. "The ox has brought us a bear. Come out and catch it!"

So the old man jumped up, tied up the bear, and threw him in the cellar.

Next morning, between dark and dawn, the old woman took her staff and drove the ox out to graze. She sat down by a mound and began spinning her flax, crying, "Graze, graze away, little ox, while I spin my flax!"

As she spun, her head drooped down, and she dozed. And lo! from out of the dark woods, a gray wolf came rushing upon the ox and said, "Who are you? Come, tell me!"

"I am a three-year-old heifer, stuffed with straw and trimmed with tar," said the ox.

"Oh, trimmed with tar, are you? Then give me some tar to tar my sides, that the dogs and the sons of dogs tear me not!"

"Take some," said the ox. And with that, the wolf fell upon him and tried to tear the tar off. He tugged and tugged and tore with his teeth, but could get none off. Then he tried to let go, but he couldn't. Tug and worry as he might, it was no good.

When the old woman awoke, there was no ox in sight. "Maybe my ox has gone home," she said.

When she got home, there stood the ox with the wolf still tugging at it. She ran and told her husband, and he came and threw the wolf into the cellar also.

On the third day, the woman again drove her ox into the pastures to graze, and sat down by a mound and dozed off.

Then a fox came running up. "Who are you?" she asked the ox.

"I'm a three-year-old heifer, stuffed with straw and covered with tar," said the ox.

"Then give me some of your tar to smear my side, for when those dogs and sons of dogs tear my hide!"

"Take some," said the ox. So the fox fastened her teeth in him. But she couldn't draw them out again.

The old woman told her husband, and he cast the fox into the cellar. After that, they caught a fat rabbit in the same way.

What do you think the old man is going to do with all the animals he threw into his cellar?

The old man sat down on a bench before the cellar and began sharpening a knife. As he did, the bear asked him, "Why are you sharpening your knife?"

"To flay your skin off, that I may make a leather jacket for myself and a cloak for my wife."

"Oh, don't flay me!" cried the bear. "Let me go, and I'll bring you lots of honey."

"Very well, see that you do it." And the old man let the bear go. Then he sat down on the bench and again began sharpening his knife. As he did, the wolf asked him, "What are you sharpening your knife for?"

"To flay off your skin, that I may make me a warm cap for the the winter."

"Oh! Don't flay me," cried the wolf. "Let me go, and I'll bring you a whole herd of woolly sheep."

"Well, see that you do it." And the old man let the wolf go. Then he sat down and began sharpening his knife again.

The fox put out her little snout, and asked him, "Why you are sharpening your knife?"

"Little foxes," said the old man, "have nice skins that make warm collars and trimmings."

"Oh! Don't take my skin away! Let me go, and I will bring you hens and geese."

"Very well, see that you do it." And the old man let the fox go. Then he sat down, and began sharpening his knife one more time.

"'Why do you do that?" asked the rabbit.

"Little hare skins will make me nice gloves and mittens for the winter!"

"Don't flay me! Let me go, and I'll bring you kale and good cauliflower!" And the old man let the rabbit go.

> *Do you think the animals will come back with what they promised?*

Then the man and his wife went to bed. Early in the morning, when it was neither dusk nor dawn, there was a noise in the doorway.

"Husband!" cried the old woman. "There's someone scratching at the door. Go and see who it is!"

The old man went out, and there was the bear carrying a

whole hive full of honey. The old man took the honey from the bear.

No sooner did he lie down than again there was a noise at the door. The old man looked out and saw the wolf driving a whole flock of sheep into the courtyard.

Close on his heels came the fox, driving before her geese and hens, and all manner of fowls. And last of all came the rabbit, bringing cabbage and kale, and all manner of good food.

The old man was glad, and the old woman was glad. And the old man sold the sheep's wool and got so rich that he needed nothing more.

As for the straw-stuffed ox, it stood in the sun till it fell to pieces.

The HOUSE ON THE HILL

Once upon a time, a curly-tailed pig said to his friend the sheep, "I am tired of living in a pen. I am going to build me a house on the hill."

"Oh! May I go with you?" said the sheep.

"What can you do to help?" asked the pig.

"I can haul the logs for the house," said the sheep.

"Good!" said the pig. "You are just the one I want. You may go with me."

As the pig and the sheep walked and talked about their new house, they met a goose.

"Good morning, pig," said the goose. "Where are you going this fine morning?"

"We are going to the hill to build us a house. I am tired of living in a pen," said the pig.

"Quack!" said the goose. "May I go with you?"

"What can you do to help?" asked the pig.

"I can gather moss, and stuff it into the cracks to keep out the rain."

"Good!" said the pig and the sheep. "You are just the one we want. You may go with us."

What could you do to help pig build a house?

As the pig and the sheep and the goose walked and talked about their new house, they met a rabbit.

"Good morning, rabbit," said the pig.

"Good morning," said the rabbit. "Where are you going this fine morning?"

"We are going to the hill to build us a house. I am tired of living in a pen," said the pig.

"Oh!" said the rabbit, with a quick little jump. "May I go with you?"

"What can you do to help?" asked the pig.

"I can dig holes for the posts of your house," said the rabbit.

"Good!" said the pig and the sheep and the goose. "You are just the one we want. You may go with us."

As the pig and the sheep and the goose and the rabbit walked and talked about their new house, they met a rooster.

"Good morning, rooster," said the pig.

"Good morning," said the rooster. "Where are you going this fine morning?"

"We are going to build us a house. I am tired of living in a pen," said the pig.

The rooster flapped his wings three times. "Oh, oh, oh, O-O-OH!" he crowed. "May I go with you?"

"What can you do to help?" asked the pig.

"I can be your clock," said the rooster. "I will crow every morning and waken you at daybreak."

"Good!" said the pig and the sheep and the goose and the rabbit. "You are just the one we want. You may go with us."

Then they all went happily to the hill.

The pig found the logs for the house. The sheep hauled them together. The rabbit dug the holes for the posts. The goose stuffed moss in the cracks to keep out the rain. And every morning, the rooster crowed to waken the workers.

When at last the house was finished, the rooster flew to the very top of it, and crowed and crowed and crowed.